**Put Beginning Readers on the Right Track with
ALL ABOARD READING™**

The All Aboard Reading series is especially designed for beginning readers. Written by noted authors and illustrated in full color, these are books that children really want to read—books to excite their imagination, expand their interests, make them laugh, and support their feelings. With fiction and nonfiction stories that are high interest and curriculum-related, All Aboard Reading books offer something for every young reader. And with four different reading levels, the All Aboard Reading series lets you choose which books are most appropriate for your children and their growing abilities.

Picture Readers

Picture Readers have super-simple texts, with many nouns appearing as rebus pictures. At the end of each book are 24 flash cards—on one side is a rebus picture; on the other side is the written-out word.

Station Stop 1

Station Stop 1 books are best for children who have just begun to read. Simple words and big type make these early reading experiences more comfortable. Picture clues help children to figure out the words on the page. Lots of repetition throughout the text helps children to predict the next word or phrase—an essential step in developing word recognition.

Station Stop 2

Station Stop 2 books are written specifically for children who are reading with help. Short sentences make it easier for early readers to understand what they are reading. Simple plots and simple dialogue help children with reading comprehension.

Station Stop 3

Station Stop 3 books are perfect for children who are reading alone. With longer text and harder words, these books appeal to children who have mastered basic reading skills. More complex stories captivate children who are ready for more challenging books.

In addition to All Aboard Reading books, look for All Aboard Math Readers™ (fiction stories that teach math concepts children are learning in school) and All Aboard Science Readers™ (nonfiction books that explore the most fascinating science topics in age-appropriate language).

All Aboard for happy reading!

Library of Congress Cataloging-in-Publication Data

Stephens, Monique Z.
  The Easter bonnet parade / by Monique Z. Stephens ; illustrated by SI Artists.
    p. cm. — (All aboard reading. Station stop 1)
"Strawberry Shortcake."
Summary: To celebrate Easter, Strawberry Shortcake and her friends decide to have an Easter bonnet parade, but what will Honey Pie Pony, who does not wear a hat, do?
  ISBN 0-448-43486-5 (pbk.)
  [1. Easter—Fiction. 2. Hats—Fiction. 3. Ponies—Fiction.] I. S.I. Artists (Group) II. Title. III. Series.
  PZ7.S83143Eas 2004
  [E]—dc22
                              2003014757

ISBN 0-448-43486-5   A B C D E F G H I J

ALL ABOARD READING™

Station Stop 1

The Easter Bonnet Parade

By Monique Z. Stephens

Illustrated by SI Artists

Grosset & Dunlap • New York

It is Easter Day
in Strawberryland.

Happy Easter,
Strawberry Shortcake!

Strawberry Shortcake has lots of Easter fun with Huckleberry Pie, Orange Blossom, Ginger Snap, Angel Cake, and Honey Pie Pony.

They make Easter baskets.

They paint Easter eggs.

They have an
Easter egg hunt!
What will they
do next?

Strawberry Shortcake
has an idea.

Let's have an Easter parade—
an Easter <u>bonnet</u> parade!

They decorate their hats.

Strawberry Shortcake

uses pretty ribbons and bows.

Orange Blossom uses
colorful paper eggs.

Angel Cake uses
bright flowers.

Ginger Snap uses wire
to make songbirds.

Huckleberry Pie uses
cotton <u>and</u> wire—
to make funny rabbit ears!

What will Honey Pie Pony use?

Wait a minute!
Honey Pie Pony
does not <u>have</u> a hat.
What will she do?

Huckleberry Pie

has a great idea.

He uses Ginger Snap's wire.

He uses Angel Cake's
bright flowers.

He uses Orange Blossom's colorful paper eggs.

He uses Strawberry Shortcake's
ribbons and bows.

He makes Honey Pie Pony
a beautiful crown!

Honey Pie Pony will be queen
of the Easter bonnet parade!

Sharing and working together
makes their Easter bonnet parade
the best parade ever.
Happy Easter, everybody!